VAMPIRE DIARY

_____

_____

Vampire Diary
A Personal Journal

Created by
Paxson Chauvet

ISBN 978-1-942790-09-9

Published by
Relentlessly Creative Books
http://relentlesslycreativebooks.com

Boulder, Colorado
USA

VAMPIRE DIARY

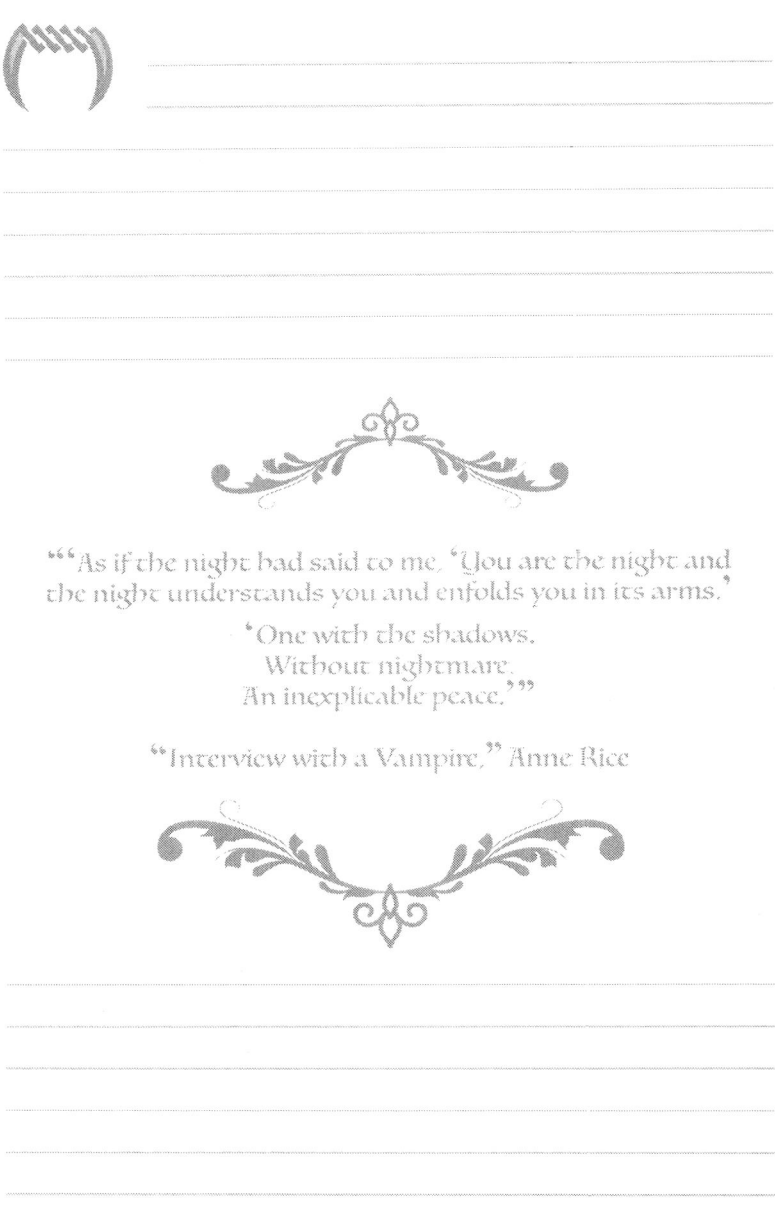

"'As if the night had said to me, 'You are the night and the night understands you and enfolds you in its arms.'

'One with the shadows.
Without nightmare.
An inexplicable peace.'"

"Interview with a Vampire," Anne Rice

"I don't know what it is about me that makes people think I want to hear their problems. Maybe I smile too much. Maybe I wear too much pink. But please remember, I can rip your throat out if I need to."

Pam, "True Blood" series, based on the "Sookie Stackhouse" novels by Charlaine Harris

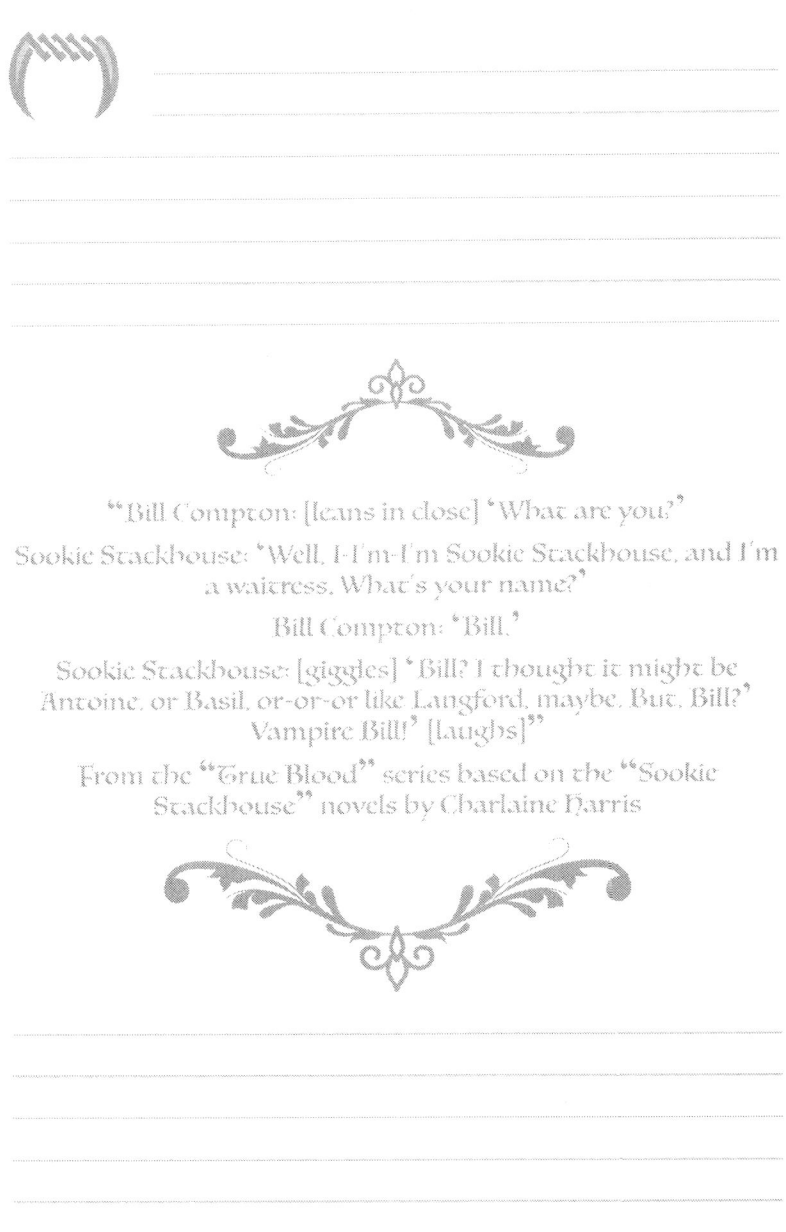

"Bill Compton: [leans in close] 'What are you?'

Sookie Stackhouse: 'Well, I-I'm-I'm Sookie Stackhouse, and I'm a waitress. What's your name?'

Bill Compton: 'Bill.'

Sookie Stackhouse: [giggles] 'Bill? I thought it might be Antoine, or Basil, or-or-or like Langford, maybe. But, Bill? Vampire Bill!' [laughs]"

From the "True Blood" series based on the "Sookie Stackhouse" novels by Charlaine Harris

"'Very few people REALLY seek knowledge in this world, few really ask. On the contrary, they try to wring from the unknown the answers they have already shaped in their own minds—justifications, confirmations, forms of consolation without which they can't go on.'

'To really ask is to open the door to the whirlwind. The answer may annihilate both the question and the questioner.'"

"Interview with a Vampire." Anne Rice

"You're going to invite me in so I can protect you, or have passionate, primal sex with you."

Eric Northman, "True Blood" series, based on the "Sookie Stackhouse" novels by Charlaine Harris

"Sookie Stackhouse: 'Can you turn into a bat?'
Bill Compton: 'No. There are those who can change form, but I'm not one of them.'

Sookie Stackhouse: 'Can you levitate?'

Bill Compton: 'No.'

Sookie Stackhouse: 'Turn invisible?'

Bill Compton: 'Sorry.'

Sookie Stackhouse: 'Well Bill, you don't seem like a very good vampire. What can you do?'

Bill Compton: 'I can bring you back to life.'"

From the "True Blood" series based on the "Sookie Stackhouse" novels by Charlaine Harris

"Loving the monsters always ends
badly for the human. It's a rule."

"Circus of the Damned."
Laurell K. Hamilton

"To make you a vampire they have to suck your
blood. And then you have to suck their blood.
It's like a whole big sucking thing."

"Welcome to the Hellmouth,"
from "Buffy the Vampire Slayer"

"He was not a vampire. Couldn't be.

'Yes, I really am one,' he murmured.

She stopped breathing. 'Can you read minds?'

'No, but I know you're staring at me, and I can
imagine how I'd feel if I were you. Look, we're a
different species, that's all.
Nothing freaky – just different.'"

From "Lover Eternal" by J.R. Ward's "Knights
of the Black Dagger Brotherhood" series

"'Has anyone ever told you how beautiful you are?' she said.

He chuckled. 'Warriors are not beautiful.'

'You are. To me. You are beautiful.'"

Beth and Wrath from the book "Dark Lover," from the Knights of the Black Dagger Brotherhood" series by J.R. Ward

"Lestat de Lioncourt – Brat prince of the kingdom
of darkness. 'Immortality is to be enjoyed, yes?
But that doesn't mean you don't have a conscience!
Listening to it... Ah, that's different!'"

"Interview with a Vampire," Anne Rice

"In the end we are alone, and there is nothing but the cold, dark wasteland of eternity."

Lestat de Lioncourt, "Interview with a Vampire," Anne Rice

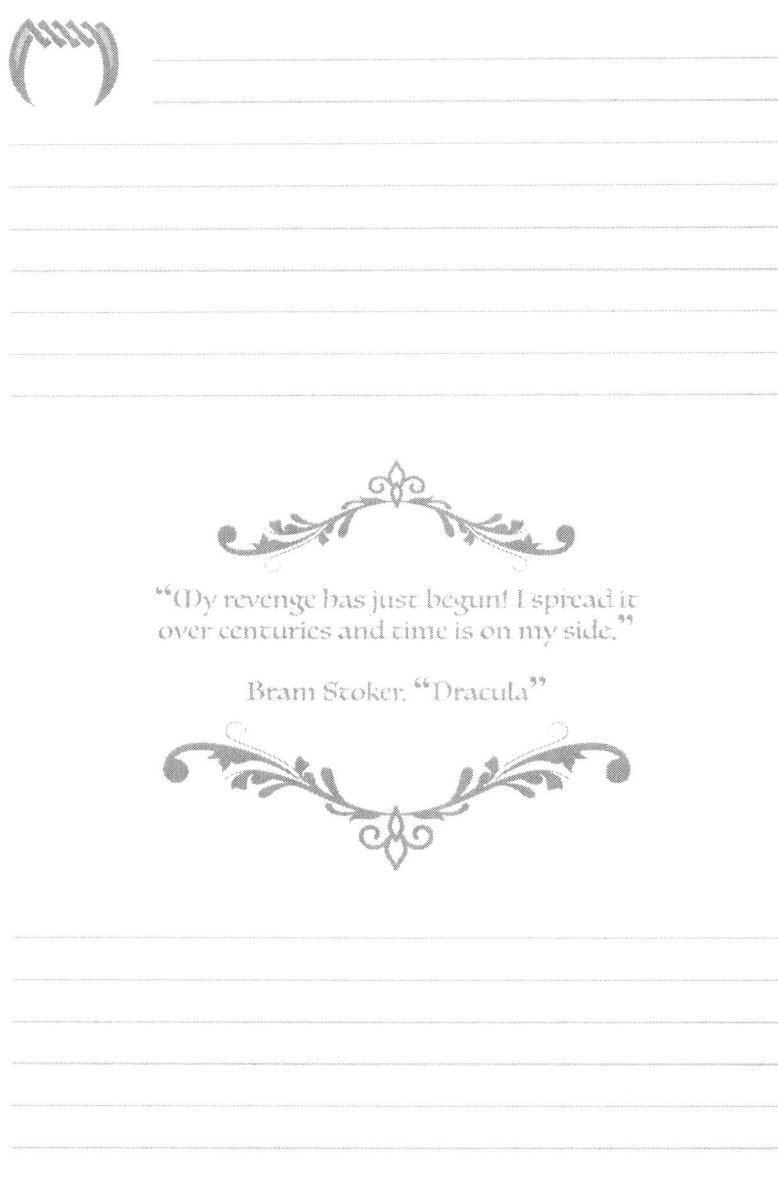

"My revenge has just begun! I spread it
over centuries and time is on my side."

Bram Stoker. "Dracula"

"Bill Compton: [to Sookie] 'We're all kept alive by magic. Sookie. My magic's just a little different from yours, that's all.'"

From the "True Blood" series based on the "Sookie Stackhouse" novels by Charlaine Harris

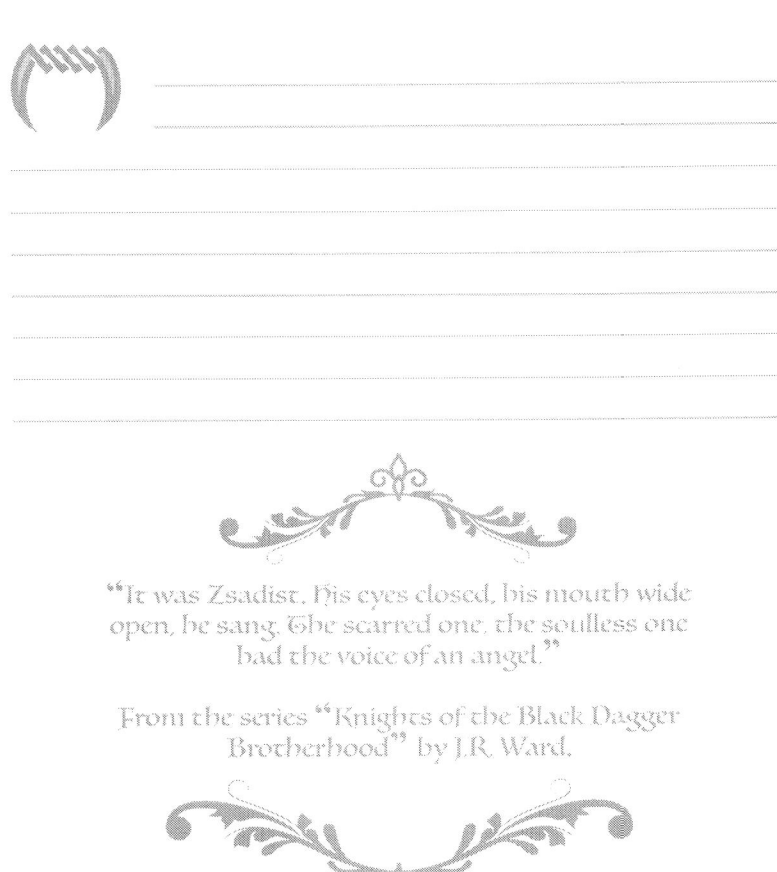

"It was Zsadist. His eyes closed, his mouth wide open, he sang. The scarred one, the soulless one had the voice of an angel."

From the series "Knights of the Black Dagger Brotherhood" by J.R. Ward.

"I came to you, Jane. Every night this week,
I didn't want you to be alone. And, I didn't
want to sleep without you."

Vishous, "Lover Unleashed," from
"Knights of the Black Dagger Brotherhood"
by J.R. Ward

"You will never grow old and you will never die."

"Interview with a Vampire," Anne Rice

"Vampires pretending to be humans
pretending to be vampires... how avant-garde!"

"Interview with a Vampire." Anne Rice

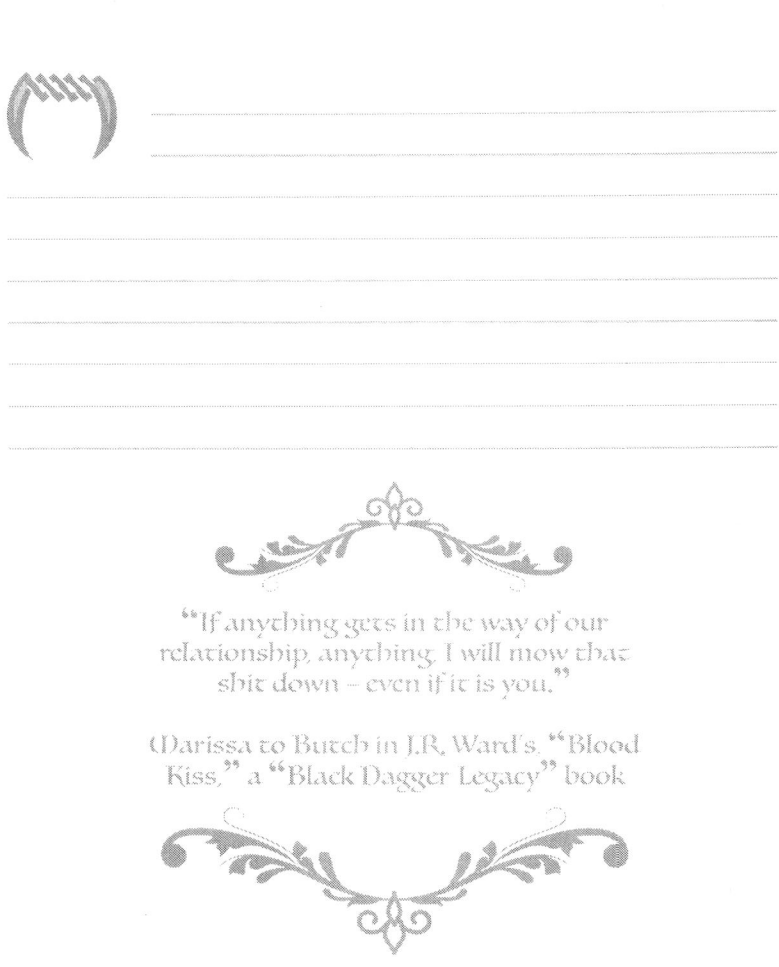

"If anything gets in the way of our
relationship, anything, I will mow that
shit down – even if it is you."

Marissa to Butch in J.R. Ward's, "Blood
Kiss," a "Black Dagger Legacy" book

"I can't help being a gorgeous fiend. It's just the card I drew."

Lestat de Lioncourt, "Interview with a Vampire," Anne Rice

"'There has to be more to life than just workin'
for the next twenty years and waitin' for a
good man to come along.'

'You need a purpose,' she said aloud
to her reflection."

Lexie Miles in "When Darkness Falls."
by Ellen Chauvet

"The blood is the life!"

Bram Stoker, "Dracula"

"You won't find a vampire in a Ford Fiesta."

Charlaine Harris, "Dead Until Dark"

"Nothing is certain, ma petite, not even death."

Jean-Claude, from the books of
Laurell K. Hamilton

"'Show me your fangs,' she demanded, thinking to trip him up.
She heard a soft click and his incisor teeth protruded
from his mouth, long and sharp.

She leapt to her feet putting distance between them. 'Thunder
crap!' but she was curious. 'Are those real?' she reached out to
touch them. Etienne remained motionless as she probed each
one. Fascinated, she tugged half expecting them to come out.

'Satisfied?' he asked. She heard a soft click
and the fangs disappeared."

Lexie and Etienne from "When Darkness Falls"
by Ellen Chauvet

Vampire Reading List

Vampire Reading List

Vampire Viewing List

Vampire Viewing List

Paxson Chauvet is the pen name of
the creators of this diary

Ellen Chauvet, author
"When Darkness Falls:
The First Vampire Redemption Story"
and
Monica Rix Paxson, author
"My Life on Earth: A Memoir"

Relentlessly
Creative
Books

Made in the USA
Columbia, SC
10 September 2017